S0-DUD-685

WITHDRAWN

Eenie Meenie Minie Moe

by Ruowen Wang
Illustrated by Wei Xu

Kevin & Robin Books
Toronto • Canada

To my family: My son, Kevin, who will read this story if I make him;
my daughter, Robin, who always reads my stories and gives her opinions;
my husband, Mike, who supports me no matter what I do;
and my 87-year-old father, Dong Chen, who can never figure out
what I do, but is proud of me for it anyway. Last but not least,
I dedicate this story to my foster mother, Anne C. Smith,
who has to make sure that whatever I do is perfectly correct.

Eenie, Meenie, Minie, Moe
Copyright © 2007 by Ruowen Wang

Published 2007 by Kevin & Robin Books
http://www.kevinandrobinbooks.com

All rights reserved. No part of this book may be reproduced or transmitted in any form or by any means, electronic or mechanical, including photocopying, recording, or any information storage and retrieval system, without permission in writing from the publisher except in the case of brief quotations embodied in critical articles and reviews.

To contact the publisher or to request permission to make copies of any part of the work, please visit Kevin & Robin Books. See website at
www.kevinandrobinbooks.com

Library and Archives Canada Cataloguing in Publication
Wang, Ruowen, 1962-
Eenie, meenie, minie, moe / written by Ruowen Wang;
illustrated by Wei Xu.

ISBN 978-0-9738798-4-1

I. Xu, Wei, 1967- II. Title

PS8645.A534E36 2007   jC813'.6
C2005-905676-2

Kevin & Robin Books

Summary: A brother and his younger sister share a bedroom. Do they take turns to keep it clean? No way! But they cannot leave it messy forever, at least not when their uncle visits. Uncle tells them a story in both English and Chinese. It starts with "Eenie, Meenie, Minie Moe," but draws upon old Chinese folklore that is both funny and wise.

First Canadian Edition 2007
Printed and bound in Hong Kong, China

Kevin and I like our uncle, Mom's older brother. Uncle is smart, funny, and a lot of fun to be with. Whenever he visits us, we have a ball. Uncle tells us stories full of funny details, crazy exaggerations, and ridiculous twists.

3

Uncle puts me on a tree branch. He is going to tell me a story. I tell him that sitting on a tree branch is a real treat for me. Uncle jokes, "If you behave well, like a lady, for the next story I will let you get up on a chimney."

"Now tell me the story please."

"Here we go! Once upon a time … No, that sounds boring, doesn't it? How would you like to listen to my improved English for a change?" Uncle came from China. He tries to speak English, and often mixes it with Chinese.

4

With his Chinese-accented English, Uncle starts again.
"Here is a better version, in English: Mini, mini, money-mole …"

He makes me laugh. "No, Uncle. It is not 'Mini, mini, money-mole.' "

"It is not 'a little money-mole'? What is it, then? That was what you taught me, wasn't it?"

"No. It should be 'Eenie, Meenie, Minie, Moe.' Now, listen carefully. Eenie, Meenie, Minie, Moe. Catch a tiger by its toe. If it hollers, let it go. Eenie, Meenie, Minie, Moe! Got it? But I thought you were going to tell me a Chinese story."

"This story I'm going to tell you is **very** Chinese. Just sit up there and listen."

"Here we go again," says Uncle. "Eenie, Meenie, Minie, Moe. Catch a monk by his toe …"

"Wrong, wrong, wrong again. It should be 'Catch a tiger by its toe.'"

"A tiger bites. It's safer to catch a monk by his toe. Now, where are we? Eenie, Meenie, Minie, Moe. Catch the monk by his toe. If he chants let him go …"

"No, no, no! You have got this part wrong too. It should be 'If it hollers, let it go'."

"Wait a minute. We are talking about a monk. Monks don't holler. Well, maybe the little monk does if his house is on fire, but the big ones chant."

"How many monks are there?"

"Three in total. Now, no more interruptions, young lady."

"But I still don't like the 'chanting' part."

"All right, whatever you say. Let's start all over again … Eenie, Meenie, Minie, Moe. Catch a monk by his toe. If he apologizes, let him go. Eenie …"

"Wait a minute! The word 'apologize' does not sound right. Why 'apologize'?"

"Well, if the monks do not do their share of the daily chores, they have to apologize. Be patient and listen to the whole story. It is a tale called 'The Three Monks,' and I will tell it to you in Chinese. I had better stop torturing you with my poor English."

A long, long time ago, in a far, far, faraway place called China, there was a small temple sitting on a mountaintop.

The hot sun was beaming down on the temple, and the cold water was shimmering below the cliff. On a winding road, up to the mountaintop walked an old monk.

Muddy sweat trickled down his face. Dirty toes peeped out of his broken shoes. It was obvious that he had walked a long way. He was tired, hungry and, above all else, extremely hot and thirsty. Finally, he reached the little temple on top of the mountain.

8

Inside the temple he found a statue of a meditating Buddha, two tall candles and a cold incense burner. A big ceramic water jar, a bamboo pole and two water buckets showed that people had lived there before.

The thirsty old monk rushed over to the water jar, but found it empty. He picked up the bamboo pole and the two buckets, and went down to the lake to fetch some water.

10

The old monk decided to make the temple his home. Month after month, he continued to live there alone. His only companion was a little mouse that came out at night to look for food and water. How the old monk longed for a human friend.

11

12

Then one day when the hot sun was beaming down on the temple, and the cold water was shimmering below the cliff, up the winding road to the mountaintop walked a tall monk.

Muddy sweat trickled down his face. Dirty toes peeped out of his broken shoes. It was obvious that he had walked a long way. He was tired, hungry and, above all else, extremely hot and thirsty. Finally he reached the little temple on top of the mountain.

Inside the temple, he found a statue of a
meditating Buddha, two tall candles and
an incense burner. A big ceramic water jar,
a bamboo pole and two water buckets
showed someone was living there.
In the middle of the floor sat an old
monk, meditating and chanting. 13

The old monk welcomed the tall monk, and offered him some cool water from the big ceramic water jar.

The tall monk drank a whole jarful of water and was very grateful. Right away, he picked up the bamboo pole and the two buckets, and headed out to fetch some more water to refill the water jar.

The old monk was happy to think that, from now on, he would have a companion and someone to fetch water.

14

After a while, the tall monk started to feel unhappy about being the only one fetching water every day. So the two monks worked out a fair arrangement: they would share the job of carrying water.

Life was perfect. It was peaceful and quiet for a while. The only disturbance was the nightly visit of the little mouse looking for food and water.

Until one day when the hot sun was beaming down on the temple, and the cold water was shimmering below the cliff, up the winding road to the mountaintop walked a little monk.

16

Muddy sweat trickled down his face. Dirty toes peeped out of his broken shoes. It was obvious that he had walked a long way. He was tired, hungry and, above all else, extremely hot and thirsty. Finally he reached the little temple on top of the mountain.

Inside the temple he found a statue of a meditating Buddha,
two candles and an incense burner. A big ceramic water jar,
a bamboo pole and two water buckets showed people were
living there. In the middle of the floor sat two monks,
meditating and chanting.

The little monk was hot and thirsty. He did not wait for his welcome, but went directly to the big ceramic water jar and held it over his head. Bottoms up!

18

The little monk finished all the water in the water jar.
Then he stretched and yawned, and was ready for a nap.

When they saw what he had done, the old monk became
very unhappy and the tall monk became very mad.

19

The old monk and the tall monk were not willing to fetch water by themselves. The little monk did not want to fetch water for the other two either. And they could not figure out how the three of them could carry water sharing one bamboo pole. From then on, each monk used a gourd containing merely enough water for his own daily use. The big ceramic water jar stayed empty.

20

21

One night, the hungry
and thirsty little mouse came
out again. Unable to find either
food or water, the little mouse climbed up a
candle and chewed it in the middle. The candle broke in half.
As the top half fell, the candle flame lit up the curtains. The
temple caught on fire!

"Fire!" The old monk jumped to his feet.

"We need water! Water!" The tall monk rushed to the big water jar.

"Help!" The little monk hollered.

22

How they wished the big water jar was full of water! Now there was no time to be sorry. The little monk and the tall monk dashed to the lake with buckets, and the old monk followed with the big water jar.

23

They all worked together to put the fire
out and save the temple.

24

From then on, the three monks shared their daily chores and lived in harmony. They even chanted in unison when meditating:

26

"Eenie, Meenie, Minie, Moe.
Catch Robin by her toe. If she
screams, don't let her go.
Eenie, Meenie, Minie, Moe."

I protest. "Hey, why me?
What have I done?"

"Well, the problem is not what
you have done, but you have
not done." My uncle lifts me off
the tree. "Come on, young lady.
Let me show you your bedroom, and then you tell
me what the problem is."

I share a bedroom with my brother, Kevin. Our bedroom is so messy that it looks like a tornado, an earthquake, and a thunderstorm have hit it all at once. No one cleans it up. Mom says it is not her bedroom. Dad says Kevin and I are both responsible. Grandpa says Mom won't let him do our job. I say my brother is older, so he should do the cleaning up. But he says if I don't do it, he won't do it either. That is how our room ends up such a mess.

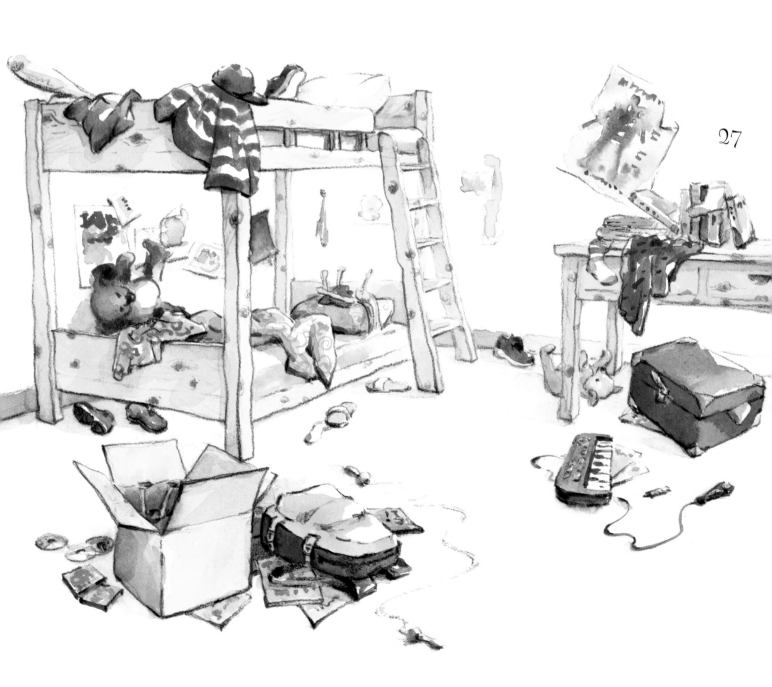

"Why should I do it? That isn't fair," I protest. "What about Kevin? Kevin has to do his part too."

"I guess you are right, young lady. All right, Kevin. Come over here. We need some justice." Uncle brings Kevin along.

"Are we going to chant 'Eenie, Meenie, Minie, Moe. Catch Kevin by his toe'?" Kevin loves this story and Uncle's silly jokes. They remind him of the good times he and Uncle spent together when he was a baby.

28

Under Uncle's supervision, Kevin and I have a fun time tidying up our room together. Uncle's crazy tales and funny jokes make doing our cleaning job painless.
We promise him that we will take turns tidying up our bedroom and will keep it clean until his next inspection.

Before Uncle leaves, he turns to us and asks, "Since you both agree to take turns tidying up your bedroom, now tell me, who is going to be the first tidy-upper?"

Kevin and I shout at the same time.

"Not me!"

"Not me!"

"Very well, then. In that case, we will just have to settle this my way." Uncle brings the two of us together, side by side. "Ready? Eenie, Meenie, Minie, Moe ..."

30

We would like to hear from you. You can contact us by email at
info@kevinandrobinbooks.com or send your letters to:

Kevin & Robin Books
64 Clancy Drive, Toronto
Ontario, Canada M2J 2V8

To obtain a copy of this book for your children, grandchildren, parents, other
family members and friends, please order online at **www.kevinandrobinbooks.com**
Be sure to check our website often. Our list of books continues to expand.
There are some ready for you now, and more are on their way.

MY GHOSTWRITER

LITTLE WEN

MY STONE LION

TO SHARE ONE MOON

GRANDPA JOE

ZIGZOO - When a Dragon Catches a Cold

AJAY

A CANADIAN IDIOT

"NEVER TRY TO OUTSAMRT A MAGICIAN"

HIDDEN TREASURES

ARE YOU THINKING WHAT I'M THINKING?

KEVIN AND ROBIN'S STORY